Francis Saltus Saltus

Flasks and Flagons

Francis Saltus Saltus

Flasks and Flagons

ISBN/EAN: 9783337083281

Printed in Europe, USA, Canada, Australia, Japan

Cover: Foto ©Andreas Hilbeck / pixelio.de

More available books at **www.hansebooks.com**

FLASKS AND FLAGONS,
PASTELS AND PROFILES,
VISTAS AND LANDSCAPES.

FRANCIS S. SALTUS.

FLASKS AND FLAGONS

PASTELS AND PROFILES   VISTAS AND LANDSCAPES

BY

FRANCIS S. SALTUS.

✠ ✠ ✠ ✠

BUFFALO
CHARLES WELLS MOULTON
1892

PRINTED BY C. W. MOULTON, BUFFALO, N. Y.

REMEMBER.

Remember me when I am gone away,
Gone far away into the silent land;
When you can no more hold me by the hand,
Nor I half turn to go, yet turning stay.

Remember me when no more day by day
You tell me of our future that you planned;
Only remember me; you understand
It will be late to counsel then or pray.

Yet if you should forget me for awhile
And afterwards remember, do not grieve;
For if the darkness and corruption leave
A vestige of the thoughts that once I had,
Better by far you should forget and smile
Than that you should remember and be sad.

CHRISTINA G. ROSSETTI.

FRANCIS S. SALTUS.

DIED JUNE 25, 1889.

A genius died last night, about whose brow
    Fame never twined the laurel and the rose.
    A master he of music, verse and prose,
Who lived, laughed, loved, and suffered, to endow

The world with buds and blossoms from the bough
    That sways within the garden where Thought grows
    When the gale of Inspiration madly blows
The daisies of sweet Song before God's plow!

Ah! who can wear the laurel, now he's dead?
    Not one among the many whom he knew!
      Pluck not the leaf for any—leave it there;
And Time will weave it for his wondrous head,
    And Fame may bear it up beyond the blue—
      To where he sits and laughs with Baudelaire!

                 JOHN ERNEST McCANN.

CONTENTS.

FLASKS AND FLAGONS.

PASTELS AND PROFILES.

CONTENTS.

VISTAS AND LANDSCAPES.

CONTENTS.

FLASKS AND FLAGONS.

BEER.

What merry fairy, oh cool, delicious beer,
   Gave thee the power through centuries to maintain
   A charm that soothes dull care, and laughs at pain;
A power sad hearts to vitalize and cheer?

No blasé palate of thy drops can fear;
   Once quaffed, lips eager, seek thy sweets again,
   Without thee students sing no loud refrain;
Laughter and mirth depart, be thou not near.

And when I drink thee to my soul's delight,
   A vision of King Gambrinus, fat and gay,
     Haunts me, and I behold bright tankards shine,
And hear him laugh with many a thirsty wight,
   And merry maiden, drinking night and day,
     In quaint, old, gabled towns along the Rhine.

B

CURACOA.

The memory haunts me, when in cheerful ease
   I sip thy sweetness, of a land of balm,
    Radiant with bowers and labyrinths of palm,
Far in the warm heart of the Celebes!

The golden orange crowns the swaying trees,
   In fertile vales there dwells perpetual calm,
    Where the swart hunter, free from any qualm,
Gazes on sultry leagues of dazzling seas.

And then strange fancy leads my spirit back
   Unto the toil and tumult of a town,
    Noisy with traffic and industrious feet.
I see the cheerless silhouette, dull and black,
   Of Rotterdam's high minster of renown,
    Or Zaandaam's markets lashed by wintry sleet!

VERMOUTH.

Thou canst unbind by potency unique,
　The tangled skein of misty souvenirs,
　And bring again, defiant of dull years,
The mantling pulse of youth unto the cheek.

Urged by thy warmth, the fancy loves to seek
　The roses of a past that disappears,
　And by some recollection that endears,
Once more, in charm, forgotten words to speak.

The sunlight of the past will then return
　Warming the soul; and I, oh blessèd boon
　　And resurrection of the things that fade,
Recall the happy days for which all yearn,
　When first I heard on Venice's lagoon,
　　The soft adagio of a serenade!

GIN.

Grim cicerone of the towns of sin,
 From thy rank drops, the germs of crime and lust,
 Nurtured by sloth and hatred of the just,
In bestial minds to awful bloom begin.

Dulling all confidence in God or kin,
 Thy woeful spectre on humanity thrust,
 Invokes sad pictures of supreme disgust,
A yelling harlot, or a bagnio's din.

I hear in St. Gilas' foulest slums, the dread
 And blasphemous cries of ruffians in mad strife,
And, the shocked eye by odious magic led,
 Sees in some garret, panting still with life,
A half-starved child clasping a woman, dead,
 While o'er them leers a gaunt brute with a knife! . .

MARASCHINO

There is a charm thy essences secrete,
  Peopling the mind with many an airy dream,
  Until in conscious pleasure it doth seem
Thy perfume hath a soul and can entreat.

So suave unto the sense, so subtly sweet,
  That memories of pre-natal beauty teem,
  And haunt the ravished brain in ways supreme,
Making our life less dark and incomplete.

I dream of the dim past, but not with pain;
  The suns of dead but resurrected years,
    Glitter once more on Venice the divine!
I see the town in bridal robes again,
  Crowned by the Doge amid his gondoliers,
    And eyes like Juliet's, softly seeking mine!

ANISETTE.

How swiftly thou canst dissipate all care
   Sweet Circe of *liqueurs*, when thou dost steal
   Our fancies from us, and with subtle zeal
Make life more rosy-tinct and debonair.

There's merry madness hidden in the air,
   Gay as the *refrain* of a Vaudeville,
   When the sweet sorcery, thou canst ne'er conceal,
Lures us to gentle laughter everywhere.

Thy very name makes resurrect to me
   The shadowy past of bygone student days;
     The *guignols*, aye, the gay cafés, and lo,
The blooming fires of youth that used to be,
   And kisses stolen in delicious ways,
     Beneath the ancestral oaks of Fontainebleau!

ABSINTHE.

Whence comes thy fatal, fascinating charm ?
  Thy fumes are sharp, dire as Medusa's tears,
  In thy green depths a tempting demon leers,
Leading the victim on without alarm.

Thy trait'rous poison makes the senses warm;
  Dull minds, grown vivid, grasp the distant spheres;
  But ah, the sad reaction, when the tears
Of madness flow, when maniac fancies swarm!

To me, thy glorious Lethe ever shows
  Some godless wretch, with haggard eyes and pale,
Seeking the shame of brutal bagnios.
  Or, mixed with powder, when all else doth fail,
  I see thee make impetuous Zouaves scale
Stern Malakoffs that teem with countless foes!

WATER.

I hear strange voices in the warm, swift rain,
   That falls in tumult upon town and field;
   It seems to tell a mystery unconcealed,
Yet hieroglyphic to a mortal's brain.

It sighs and moans as if in utter pain
   Of some colossal sorrow, never healed;
   It warns of awful secrets unrevealed,
And every drop repeats the sad refrain.

And then I think of the enormous sea
   Fed by these drops, with drifting wrecks bestrewn,
     And dimly, vaguely, like a far-off sound,
The meaning of their sorrow comes to me,
   For they may be, oh rare, considerate boon,
     Heaven's humble mourners for the unnumbered
       drowned.

AMONTILLADO.

When thy inspiring warmth pervades my frame,
  I see the smiling Guadalquiver stray
  Through Andalusia's fields of endless May,
Crowned by the ripe wheat like a golden flame.

The majos sport in many a wanton game
  At the soft setting of the ardent day,
  And in the Alameda's shadows gray,
Fond lovers murmur their delicious shame.

And then again, the vision will arise
  Before me, of the worn Campeador
    Draining thy fire beneath the Alhambra's stars,
While with fierce Moslem-valor in their eyes,
  I see bejeweled Caliphs, red with gore,
    Battle to death in moated Alcazars!

C

KIRSCH.

The mysteries of the Schwarzwald in thee dwell!
　　Thou must be made in hidden fairies' homes,
　　Deep in dim glades, where, in the midnight roams
The sable Huntsman on his ride to hell!

Thy drops must aid red witches to foretell
　　Their awful secrets in unholy tomes,
　　And in the haunted dusk, the limping gnomes,
Meeting near somber firs, must know thee well.

To me, thou art associate ever more
　　With beldames' legends of the weird, blue Rhine,
　　　Where white and wanton nixes bathe themselves.
I see thee luring travelers to the shore,
　　While in the gloomy forest near them shine
　　　The lurid eyes of hell-obeying elves!

LAMBIC.

Lips that first taste thy asper charm are shy;
　Thou art not lightly wooed to prove a friend,
　But, when all hesitations surely end,
How finely, fully, dost thou satisfy!

The sturdy essences that in thee lie,
　With fumes tumultuous to the brain ascend,
　And with a Herculean vigor rend
All lingering doubts and force their passage by.

And when I drink thee in some gabled inn,
　Deep in the alleys of a Flemish town,
　　While buxom villagers around me romp,
I hear old, garrulous crones again begin
　The story all of wonder and renown,
　　That still keeps green the laurels of Van Tromp!

BASS'S ALE.

Whene'er thy foaming beads attract my lips,
  A rapid vision passes o'er my mind
  Of strong Cunarders, battling with the wind,
And cosy cabins, and the roll of ships.

I hear the tempest lash the sails like whips,
  I see the rigid bow its pathway find
  Deep in the night, leaving in sheen behind
A snaky trail of phosphorescent tips.

Or, when thy vigor to the lees I drain,
  I, from the belfry of St. Paul's behold
    Gigantic London in gray winter hours,
Waiting for drowsy dawn to come again,
  While the great sun, veiled in a fog of gold,
    Bursts in red glory on her haughty Towers!

BRANDY.

Thy mighty power stirs up the sluggish blood
  To craft and cunning and rejuvenate fire,
  And fills again with raptures of desire
The failing sense that drowns in amour's flood.

The spirit's song, freed from our carnal mud,
  Then soars supreme, and grandlier doth aspire,
  And with new vigor that can never tire,
The flowers of fancy burst within the bud.

In nobler ways, even yet, thou prov'st thy might,
  When soldiers, strengthened by thy drops of flame
    Forget their gory wounds in frantic zeal,
And with high souls all thrilling for the fight,
  Assault dread bastions for their country's fame,
    And lead their flags thro' labyrinths of steel!

KÜMMEL

Thy acrid fumes my laggard sense excite,
  There's war and wrangle hidden in thy heart
  That make one's breast with expectation start,
Eager to seek armed enemies to smite.

Thy savor is a danger and delight,
  For those of valorous souls, the favorite art,
  Thy fire with all mine own becomes a part,
I yearn to battle madly for the right.

And on far Ukraines' snowy steppes I see
  Pale, shackled Poles to far Siberia led,
    Torn from the gentle pleasance of their homes,
And then I yearn to hasten and to free
  Their hands, and trample upon Cossack dead,
    Beneath the shade of Nijnis' golden domes!

TOKAI.

A glass of thy reviving gold to me,
  Whether or no my dreamy soul be sad,
  Brings souvenirs of lovely Vienna, glad
In her eternal summer-time to be!

I hear, in joyous trills, resounding free,
  The waltzes that the German fairies bade
  The souls of Strauss and Lanier, music mad,
Compose, to set the brains of worlds aglee.

And in the Sperl, dreaming away the sweet
  Of pleasant life, and finding it all praise,
    Dead to the past and scorning Death's surprise,
I see in calm felicity complete
  Some fair Hungarian Jewess on me gaze,
    With the black glory of Hebraic eyes!

BÉNÉDICTINE.

Born in the cloistral solitude and gloom
  Of gray La Trappes and monasteries drear,
  Distilled between the matin mass austere
And drearier Vespers, thou dost humbly bloom.

The damp, chill crypts a lighter guise assume,
  And, with thy soothing perfume, disappear
  Grim thoughts of death and of diurnal fear,
While rosy glamours hover o'er the tomb!

And when I sip thy cloying sweets, they bring
  A faith, not wholly lost, unto my heart;
    I trust again the twitter of the birds;
Sweet voices as of angels to me sing,
  And strengthened, holier, I can live apart,
    Finding new beauty in the Savior's words.

CHAMBERTIN.

The blackest skies are bright when thou art near;
   Pain is a myth, and sorrow a refrain;
   Life, blood and vigor spurtle in each vein,
And even the lurking tomb is no more drear.

The joyous heart knows naught of Autumn's sere,
   In woman's kiss there is no hidden bane;
   The monarch of the land deserves his reign,
The poor have rubies and all life is dear!

Alas, 'tis but a dream; yet, from thee came
   The prowess of Napoleon the Great,
     Who loved thee while his conquered foes did yield.
From thee was born fierce Borodinos' flame,
   Jenas' stupendous charge of deathly hate,
     And the red ruin of Marengo field!

D

GEISENHEIMER.

Thy laughing gold could steal the sense away
   From gravest counselors and statesmen stern,
   And with thy haunting redolence could learn,
The secrets of a Bismarck or Touché.

Hearts closed by giant will would thee obey
   And babble gaily, aye, to prate would burn,
   Guilt would confess beyond all life's return,
And naked truth would revel for a day.

Therefore I dread thy cunning, and with care
   Content myself with dreams when thou art near,
   Checking the idle word that idly slips,
For by thy charm, who knows, when unaware,
   I might divulge the name I hold most dear,
    And all the passionate secrets of her lips?

PORT.

When unto me they bring, with gentle care,
　　Thy nectar, sleeping in the cobwebbed flask,
　　There is no boon of fairy gods to ask
More pain annihilating or more rare.

The gloomy gray of storm-clouds seemeth fair,
　　Thou makest light the long day's onerous task,
　　Uplifted lies life's tedium and its mask,
Light, love and laughter enter everywhere.

And then I see old bankers, flushed with pride,
　　Converse on politics, and gold, and Pitt;
　　　But cheerier far, in some dim tavern's nook,
I see in dreams dear Jerrold, by the side
　　Of glorious Thackeray, listening to the wit,
　　　And gay, infectous laugh of Theodore Hook!

RUM PUNCH.

The world to give thee lasting fame combines,
  Jamaica sends thee sugar-cane, o'er seas;
  And pungent spices from the Antilles,
Lend thee the perfumes of the southern vines.

France gives the crimson sorcery of her wines,
  Mongolia lavishes her yellow teas,
  And to endower thee with rare mysteries,
Sicily yields her lemons and sweet pines.

Thou dost recall to me days debonair,
And visions of the Quartier Latin, where,
  Chatting around thy bluish spectral light,
    Insouciant students and alert grisettes
    Drank thee while puffing *régie* cigarettes,
  Mocking with merry song the startled night!

CHATEAU MARGAUX.

There is a power within the succulent grape
   That made thee, stronger than all human power.
   It baffles death in its exulting hour,
And leaves its victim fortune to escape.

Thy cheering drops can magically drape
   Atrocious thoughts of doom with bloom and flower,
   Turning to laughing calm care's torment sour,
And flooding dreams with many a gentle shape.

Extatic hope and resurrection lie
   In thy consoling beauty, and whene'er
     Pale mortals sip thee, bringing soothing peace,
I see a blue and orange-scented sky,
   A warm beach blest by God's untainted air,
     Circling the snowy parapets of Nice!

CHARTREUSE VERT.

How strange that thy enrapturing warmth should come
　From the chill cloister of the prayerful monk,
　To cheer the desolate heart in misery sunk,
And warm the lips that sorrow has made dumb!

Thou bring'st the merry twitter of birds that hum,
　The soul's sweet exodus of song, when shrunk
　Expands again, when, all thy sweetness drunk,
Illumes the blood grown impotent and numb.

And when I see thee, I most fondly dream
　Thou must have been the genius and the slave
　　That led Aladdin in the legend old
Down thro' dim passages to goals extreme,
　And in the arcana of a hidden cave
　　Have shown him marvelous treasuries of gold!

IRISH WHISKEY.

From Cork to Tipperary and Tralee,
  There's been more laughter, jollity and fun
  Than yet's been known beneath the risen sun
In all the world together, born of thee!

Thou bring'st out finely the old Celtic glee,
  Yarns, jokes and glorious bulls surpassed by none,
  Side-splitting stories, funny when begun,
And at the end one royal mental spree.

And when I drink thee quite alone, ('tis rare),
  I picture up a host of merry men,
    Tasting thy charm and joking without stint,
And recognize the Hoods and Jerrolds there
  Who, gay and careless, never take a pen,
    But cast their gems beyond the grasp of print!

SCOTCH WHISKEY.

How rare is thy rich, passion-giving worth,
  When weary of full many a Scottish mile,
  One rests, and stirs thee with a knowing smile
In some dim inn of Edinburgh or Perth.

Gods must have drunk thee at their wondrous birth,
  For in thee there is laughter and no guile,
  And they, enraptured, from some heavenly aisle,
Perchance have given thee to this sorrowing earth.

For when thou art near, the devil has the pain,
  No bitter frown is known, no caustic sneer,
    The world on golden axles moves and turns.
And then ring out again, and yet again,
  In manly accents, resolute and clear
    The immortal songs and glees of Bobby Burns!

MENTHE.

There is in thee a chill taste of the tomb,
    A strange and perfumed warning of decay,
    Thou warmest not, and yet thou canst allay,
For a brief span, all fantasies of gloom.

Then does the fancy sadder garb assume,
    One wearies of the freshness of the May,
    The dead seem nearer and poison the fair day,
On light and feathery clouds there hangs a doom.

I see when thou art near the fresh-dug graves
    Of wan consumptives by the North fog spread,
      Beside some mournful beach where dull waves curl;
Or sadder still, when hope no longer saves,
    I see some self-slain bankrupt, lying dead
      Within the boudoir of a Cora Pearl!

E.

ARRACK.

I see a sultry land of palm and rice
  Haunted by upas and malarial dust,
  Whene'er against the chilling world unjust
I drink thy fire, oblivion to entice.

Vistas of pagan gods of strange device,
  Mysterious worship and atrocious lust,
  Arise and linger, on my memory thrust
With sounds of gongs and burnings of sweet spice.

I see in Java's forests, when the night
  Burns all alive with stars, the savage priests
    Draining thy fire, with fragrant essence oiled;
I see each motion weird, each awful rite
  When by thee drunk they sacrifice fell beasts
    And dance with cobras on nude bosoms coiled!

CHAMPAGNE FRAPPÉ.

Delicious, effervescent, cold Champagne,
   Imprisoned sunshine, glorious and bright,
   How many virtues in thy charm unite?
Who from thy tempting witchery can abstain?

Sad hearts by *ennui* vexed revive again
   When in the frail, green glass thou foamest light,
   And by thy spell our sophistry takes flight;
Fair queen of wines, long be thy merry reign.

To me thy sparkling souvenir recalls
   Grand Boulevards, all dazzling with the glare
      Of countless lights; the revel and uproar
Of midnight Paris and the Opera balls;
      A maze of masks! a challenge flung to Care!
         And charming suppers at the " Maison d'Or!"

TEA.

From what enchanted Eden came thy leaves
  That hide such subtle spirits of perfume?
  Did eyes pre-adamite first see thee bloom,
Luscious nepenthe of the soul that grieves?

By thee the tired and torpid mind conceives,
  Fairer than roses brightening life's gloom,
  Thy protean charm can every form assume
And turn December nights to April eves.

Thy amber-tinted drops bring back to me
  Fantastic shapes of great Mongolian towers,
    Emblazoned banners, and the booming gong;
I hear the sound of feast and revelry,
  And smell, far sweeter than the sweetest flowers,
    The kiosks of Pekin, fragrant of Oolong!

CHOCOLATE

Liquid delectable, I love thy brown
　Deep-glimmering color like a wood-nymph's tress;
　Potent and swift to urge on Love's excess,
Thou wert most loved in the fair Aztec town

Where Cortes, battling for Iberia's crown,
　First found thee, and with rough and soldier guess,
　Pronounced thy virtues of rare worthiness
And fit by Madrid's dames to gain renown.

When tasting of thy sweets, fond memories
　Of bygone days in Versailles will arise;
　　Before the King, reclining at his ease
I see Dubarry in rich toilet stand,
　A gleam of passion in her lustrous eyes,
　　A Sevres cup held in her jeweled hand!

COFFEE.

Voluptuous berry! where may mortals find
  Nectars divine that can with thee compare,
  When, having dined, we sip thy essence rare,
And feel towards wit and repartee inclined?

Thou wert of sneering, cynical Voltaire
  The only friend; thy power urged Balzac's mind
  To glorious effort; surely Heaven designed
Thy devotees superior joys to share.

Whene'er I breathe thy fumes, 'mid Summer stars,
  The Orient's splendent pomps my vision greet.
    Damascus with its myriad minarets gleams!
I see thee, smoking, in immense bazars,
  Or yet in dim seraglios, at the feet
    Of blonde Sultanas, pale with amorous dreams!

,

LACHRYMA CHRISTI.

There is a sadness in their very name,
　Chosen by holy monks in ways unknown.
　Thou dost refresh, but, ah! not that alone,
Dull wormwood lingers in thy ruddy flame.

Made warm by thee, the heart feels full of shame,
　The merry birds of jocund thought have flown,
　And, as by magic, meditative grown,
The mind no more can peace or pleasure claim.

For then I dream that in departed years,
　On Calvary when the dark day was drear,
　　Shrouded by angry Heaven's supreme eclipse,
Thou, to assuage the suffering Savior's tears,
　Wert brutally tendered on a Roman spear,
　　In the foul sponge that withered his sweet lips!

PASTELS AND PROFILES.

CHARLES II.

ENGLAND.

A gay and brilliant court makes sport of care;
   A merry monarch revels with his kin;
   Delicious, flower-like women bloom within
Proud, stately halls, that teem with paintings rare.

Rochester, wigged and curled, has striven to win
   The royal smile, while young and debonair,
   Charles smooths his favorite spaniel's flossy hair,
And jests behind a screen with pert Nell Gwynn.

Without, the sad town slumbers mute and dire;
   The fleets of Holland in the gray Thames rest;
A starving people, mad by woe and ire,
   Breathe the foul air still haunted by the pest,
And hear with blanchened cheeks and hearts oppressed,
   Grave, ominous bells of brass that warn of fire!

F

LOUIS XIV.

FRANCE.

The world recalls thee, monarch, in thy state
  And purple pomp of court; it sees thee stand,
  Ermined and blazoned o'er with gold, and grand,
While Europe's princes on thy bidding wait.

Turenne in war baptized thy name as great,
  Versailles arose from naught at thy command,
  But thou, oh king, a scepter in thy hand,
Didst use as bludgeon its imperial weight.

I dream of thy dead reign in other ways,
  When thou wert greatly blessed, before a care
Had gloomed thy heart, and see thee, to thy praise,
  Gallant and beautiful, with talents rare,
In the sweet, sunny summer of thy days,
  Kissing the fawn-like eyes of La Vallière.

FRANCIS I.

FRANCE.

A dazzling banquet-hall at Rambouillet,
  A gold-crushed board flowing with spice and wine,
  On silk and gems and burnished armor shine,
The love-lit eyes of Diane de Poictiers.

From cups Cellini-chiseled, proud and gay,
  The king quaffs deep unto their rays divine,
  And while composing his rondel's last line,
Laughs at the ribald jests of Triboulet.

   *   *   *   *   *   *

The field of Pavia glitters with the slain,
  A king is there, by tides of foemen tossed,
His reeking glaive cleaveth thro' casque and brain,
  A hundred lances on his breast are crossed,
While bleeding and weak he cries with pride and pain,
  " All but my knightly honor now is lost!"

PETER THE GREAT.

RUSSIA.

Hero of iron, cast in a giant's mould,
　Thy brow was formed for crowns, thy hands to sway,
　From Finland to the Caspian's waves, and weigh
The destinies of nations young and bold.

Knight, warrior, statesman, genius uncontrolled,
　Profound in council, reckless in the fray,
　Thy soul prophetic doubted not the day
When thy trained legions toward Pultava rolled.

And when I ponder on thy mighty deeds,
　Majestic visions float before mine eyes
　　Of dismal, blood-stained steppes and burning homes,
Swedish hussars falling from maddened steeds,
　And all the clash of steel 'mid conquering cries
　　Beneath great Kremlins and Byzantine domes!

HENRY IV.

FRANCE.

"Long live our king, good Harry of Navarre!"
  Shouted the soldiery through Ivry's heat;
  Thou led'st them on to victory complete,
Proud in the glamour of thy Huguenot star!

Good king, thy glorious deeds immortal are;
    France, old in years, thy memory still doth greet,
    And peasants love thy great name to repeat,
Sapient in council, valorous in war.

I see thy Béarn face as histories tell,
    Frank, open, winning, resolutely free;
I see thee armed with helmet and poitrel.
    And then again, in thy broad Tuilerie,
    I hear thy joyous oath "Ventre-saint-Grés,"
And see thee kiss thy swan-necked Gabrielle!

CHRISTINA.

SWEDEN.

A wondrous Queen wert thou all men will own,
   Proud scion of the grim, old, troublous Norse;
   Whether in robes of state, or on thy horse
Leading men battleward, thy genius shone.

Thy soul patrician yearned not for a throne,
   But bloomed for Art and Lore, and found new force
   When, leaving icy realms without remorse,
It sought the joys of Italy alone.

Yet wise men say thy abdication's shame
   Was fear-inspired, and that by danger pressed
Thou spurnedst the crown! but history will proclaim
   That thy pure, regal blood no dread confessed.
Let men who doubt, look to thy queenly name
   Signed with a sword in Monaldeschi's breast!

CHARLES I.

ENGLAND.

Son of the haughty, antique Stuart stock,
  Aristocratic in such fatal ways,
  Thy people saw no new and pleasant days
Dawn by thy rule; unyielding as a rock.

To grant just laws thy impatient soul would shock;
  Alas! thou couldst not delve thro' treachery's maze,
  Nor lull in time the Revolution's blaze
That lit thy royal pathway to the block.

I see thee in that court of high repute,
  Gazing upon thy judges in surprise,
Switching with careless hand thy Spanish boot,
  Scorning the mob's foul jibes and angry cries;
While lo! behind an arras hidden and mute,
  Stern Cromwell watches thee with lurid eyes!

MONTEZUMA.

MEXICO.

Imperial Aztec, lord of valleys, where
   Proud Tenochtitlau's palaces and bowers,
   Girt by chinampas of delicious flowers,
Rose in white symmetry in the sunlight fair.

You failed to guess the crafty Spaniard's snare,
   You lacked a faith in Quetzacoatl's powers,
   And so your people perished in the showers
Of leaden hail because you would forbear!

Whene'er your name, poor martyr, greets mine eye,
   I see in revels of carnage and of pain,
   Slate maquahuitls thud and oak bows strain,
And hear of Cortes the victorious cry,
While o'er the grim, burnt teocollis fly
   The torn, emblazoned bannerets of Spain!

MARY TUDOR.

BLOODY MARY.

Oh heartless queen, as orthodox as chaste,
   Didst thou not weary of the famine-fire
   Fed with sad martyr flesh that dared aspire
Only to gracious God ? whose pangs disgraced

Thy dawning reign, and for all time effaced
   The glorious deeds and valor of thy sire ?
   Wert thou of Nero blood that could not tire
To view foul slaughter on a desolate waste ?

Whene'er I think of thee, I see grim men,
   Masked to the chin within the Tower-hall stand.
Thy cherished Philip was morose again.   .   .
   Spurned British lioness, in thy fury grand,
I watch thee sign death warrants with swift pen,
   And doom a life with one wave of thy hand.

G

LOUIS XVI.

FRANCE.

A livid throng surrounds thy Tuileries,
  A famished people, armed with gory spikes,
  Treads on the ancient crown of its dislikes,
Rushing upon the palace like great seas,

In untamed fury, and thou hast no dykes
  Of steel and cannon to stop men like these!
  It needs more lenient treatment to appease
And curb an outraged nation when it strikes!

Poor, helpless king, thou couldst expect no grace
  From men who taunting thee with insults keen,
Resolved thy royal lineage to efface,
  And doom thy life, thy court, thy son, thy queen!
Until the crimes of the whole Bourbon race
  Were purged in blood upon the guillotine!

FREDERICK THE GREAT.

PRUSSIA.

Keen, silky ruse unsheathed your heart of stone,
　You hid sharp tiger-claws among your lords.
　When soft words failed, with sudden shock of swords,
To gain the prize your arm staked life and throne.

Intolerant Austria, rent by grave discords,
　Despised your rising star, and left alone
　Her fair Silesian rose, to find it prone,
Ravished and crushed by your invading hordes.

But when in dreams your memory steals to me,
　I watch you amid your clamorous dogs repair
To some old, sombre room at Sans Souci,
　To play upon the flute a favorite air,
And, by your side, I see, in devilish glee
　The mocking smile and cold sneer of Voltaire!

MARIE STUART.

SCOTLAND.

Sweet, prayerful martyr of the sullen days,
  When grim old London lingered in the gloom
Of frowning gibbets and of pyres, whose blaze
  Was fed by flesh, and when the Tower-bell's boom

Rang forth a knell lugubrious thro' dark ways!
  When love, and sin, and crime found one same tomb,
  Remember Queen, thy odious, hurried doom,
Hath found in history an avenging praise.

The cold, sharp axe that smote thy regal head
  Sundered not with it thy poetic breath,
For, thro' long ages that have waned and fled,
  We guard thy name that ne'er will know of death,
While thy pure blood still spatters with its red,
  The hideous wrinkles of Elizabeth!

FRANCIS II.

FRANCE.

Your cruel mother, fiend of rack and rope,
  Blood-bathed your crown, for she divined your reign
  Would be but brief, a turmoil and a pain;
Foul superstition gave her soul no hope.

Her necromancers drew your horoscope,
  Wooing sad planets, but ne'er sought again,
  The Valois star hung heavy on the wane,
And Catherine's will with Fate dared never cope.

But, while she trembled, what cared you, oh king!
  When life was sweet, tho' stained by bloody blots;
You had loud right to love the rosy spring,
  To shun the church, the mass, the Huguenots,
And you were wise to make good cheer, and sing
  The lays of France with your white Queen of Scots.

HENRY III.

FRANCE.

Effeminate king, the gold weight of thy crown
   Was far too massive for thy nerveless brows;
   Not in wild war but in long, lewd carouse,
Did thy misspent reign reap its dull renown.

Thy frizzled pups, the damozels of thy house,
   Absorbed thy vagrant thoughts, poor sceptred clown,
   And the feigned anger of thy royal frown,
Awed not thy mignons at their midnight bouse.

When curled and sashed, and in thy raiment dressed,
   Thy lean buffon a nobler mien hath shown,
The antique grandeur of the Valois crest,
   Gleamed lordlier on his satin than thine own.
He was the king, yet thou didst let his jest
   Come with coarse laugh to mock thy very throne.

PHARAOH.

EGYPT.

Monarch o'er countless leagues of palm and sand,
  What are to thee an unknown God's decrees?
  Numberless as thy sphinx's granite gries,
The hosts of Egypt wait thy first command.

Thou scorn'st the plagues that desolate thy land,
  The awful darkness and the foul disease;
  With thy first-born clasped dead upon thy knees,
I see thee gaze, inflexible and grand!

Whene'er I hear thy puissant name, I dream
  Of tapering obelisks and festal halls,
    Bathed by the lotused Nile; the pomp and awe
Of Phtâ's dim temples where gold altars gleam,
  And, beneath Pyramids where the fierce sun falls,
    I see pale, haggard Hebrews toil with straw.

LOUIS XI.

FRANCE.

We see thee in thy many-bastioned Plessis,
  Tortured by mental pangs beyond all healing,
  Abject before thy leaden virgins kneeling,
Praying and weeping as grim death progresses.

Fearing thy son, yet loving his caresses,
  Suspicious tyrant in thy hard heart stealing,
  Dawns there no tender thought, no Christian feeling,
For all the guileless folk thy hand oppresses?

Nay, thou hast care but for the crown thou'rt wearing;
  Pity would rob thy power of its ascendant;
And still the horrid rack goes on unsparing.
  Astounded Death has found a new intendant;
Touraine resounds with sighing and despairing,
  And thou canst count a corpse from each tree pendent.

PHILIP II.

The Escurial frowns upon the great blue night.
  Oh king thou standest there, in calm, alone!
  What do thy sad thoughts tell the listening stone?
Do not the phantoms of thy youth's delight

Loom up and haunt thee? I can hear thee moan
  And gnaw thine ashen lips with creeping fright;
  Philip, the shades that flit before thy sight,
Are they of friends that perished for thy throne?

No, no, tho' hidden by thy granite's gloom,
  Faces more hideous haunt thy mind and stay.
Not they who in battle found an honored tomb,
  Not they who died in Indias far away,
The souls that haunt thee, thou, thyself didst doom
  To die in fire at thine Auto-da-fé!

H

LOUIS XIII.

FRANCE.

Thou couldst not bear with its gigantic weight,
  Thy royal father's fame indeed, but thou,
  Puniest of kings, heldst on thy sallow brow,
The mighty laurels none dared desecrate.

Of Richelieu, puissant in his love and hate
  Who knelt before thee, but who made thee bow
  Thy anointed head; this is thy glory now:
A twirl of scarlet made or marred thy state.

Yet history lenient in caressing ways,
  Tells of lewd courts, where thou wert forced to dwell,
And of thy chastity unto thy praise
  And no encompassed king loved France so well
As thou didst, and thy foes recall the days
  When thy strong glaive hung over La Rochelle.

HAROUN–AL–RASCHID.

ARABIA.

Hail, glorious Caliph of the dear, dead days!
  In your domains Art blossomed strong, secure!
  Wise were your lips, noble your heart and pure,
Your worthy reign was one of utter praise.

In merchant's garb disguised, with black Mesrour,
  You threaded lovely Bagdad's inner ways,
  To see your people at their tasks and plays,
To guard the innocent and to bless the poor.

Whene'er of your magnificence I dream,
  The luminous Orient rises proud and bright.
I see grand Mosques and minarets that gleam,
  Saracen warriors rushing to the fight!
Vast, turbaned hosts, banners that wave and stream,
  One mighty revel of color, pomp and light!

CHARLES V.

SPAIN.

Your steel-clad hosts, eager to conquer spheres,
  O'er Flemish snows, and desert sands unfurled
  The banner of Spain, tattered and torn and curled,
Floating in glory through unnumbered years.

Your look was flame, your very name bred fears;
  Within your hand trembled the shackled world,
  And Europe's chaos by your will was hurled
Back into symmetry with a thousand spears.

Statesman and conqueror, soldier, prince, we own
  That you were born to curb, command, and crush,
But when I summon you, to my mind alone,
  One glorious act of yours will ever rush,
When, with great Titian, heedless of your throne,
  You knelt to pick up his immortal brush.

LAUZUN.

FRANCE.

Pet of a reign unequaled in its splendor,
   Supremely beautiful and debonair,
   Rich as a Crœsus, witty as Voltaire,
Whose heart before thy grace would not surrender.

The haughty court-dames elegantly slender,
   Flowers of Versailles, visions of radiance fair,
   Were proud to brook thy insolence, and share
The sweet enchantments of thy glances tender.

Of crime or treachery holding no alarms,
   Through that grand epoch, pale with love's excesses,
I see thee pass with fascinating charms,
   Receiving ever honors and caresses,
From august Louis, or the enamored arms
   Of pert soubrettes and powdered marchionesses.

ATTILA.

SCYTHIA.

Of Scythian wastes proud undisputed lord,
   You led your blue-eyed stalwart Huns, whose cries
   Of brutal joy and uncontrolled surprise,
Hailed Rome a vassal to your conquering sword!

But golden ransoms in your coffers poured;
   You that were named the scourge of God, unwise,
   Duped by a Valentinian of the prize,
At victory's gates withdrew your impatient horde!

Whene'er my mind is haunted by your name
   I see the Roman streets ablaze with light!
Your advent, white-haired senators proclaim,
   All is confusion, consternation, fright!
The guard Protorian buckles for the fight,
   And the great city burns with rage and shame!

LOUIS XV.

FRANCE.

A dream of Watteau was thy merry reign,
  Reveling in witty song, gay foe to care;
Warm was the wine at Folly's feast insane,
  That pledged the court-dames' pastel-beauty rare.

Age of the dainty *mouche*, the powdered hair,
  Of gallant *abbés*, poodles, balls, chicane,
Of ribbons, intrigues, duels, Parc aux Cerfs,
  Fond age of pleasure trampling upon pain.

Thy name, oh king, brings to my mind a glow
  Of those bright days that ravish and allure;
I see Dubarry's golden goblet flow
  With sparkling foam, like to her wit as pure,
Or I can hear thy *blasé* whisperings, low,
  Behind the ivory fan of Pompadour.

CHARLES XII.

SWEDEN.

The star that glittered on thy natal day,
  Illumed thy path and taught thee to succeed;
  It led thy legions on, impetuous Swede,
O'er Polish snows to conquer and to slay.

It followed thee unto that gloomy way,
  Where Norse and Goth made the dark Neva bleed,
  And where the Russian sceptre like a reed,
Was snapped in Narva's desolating fray.

But northern mists then veiled it from thy sight;
  Thou didst not see the Czar's advancing hordes;
Giant! before thou couldst turn back to smite,
  With riot of cannon and with clash of swords,
Thy great star, glittering in the Norway night
  Fell with a shudder in the frozen fjords!

CHARLES IX.

FRANCE.

The Louvre guarded to its outer gate,
   Bristles with halberds; the great culverin
Booms o'er the town; deep-lunged and desolate,
   The iron tocsin clangs o'er flame and din;

While thou, pale king, nurtured by gall and hate,
   Pantest within thine alcove, when begin
   The monstrous murders, offspring of thy sin,
Staining with infamy thy crown and state.

On that mad, tigerish night of pain and loss,
   How was thy sleep, king? Were thine eyes not wet
With fiercest tears as on thy couch didst toss?
   Didst thou not see in dreams of vast regret,
A Huguenot Christ nailed to a martyr's cross
   Flooding thy France in drops of bloody sweat?

1

HENRY VIII.

ENGLAND.

The Tower looms grim, see of your reign the fruit
   Vile king! an hapless folk is doomed to flame,
   You hear the oak pyres burn, the royal name
Gains by such needless anguish no repute.

Bigoted fool, seed of a bigot root,
   Do you not hear the tortured victims claim
   Another throne in hell for you, of shame
Fit for your carrion! soulless, sceptred brute?

You cared but little for a dead man's bones.
   Meseems through history's mists, they gave no pain,
But should you deem your butcher prayer atones
   For all the slaughter of your impious reign,
Remember king, pale Howard's dying groans;
   Think of the axe that smote poor Ann Boleyn.

CÆSAR.

ROME.

Thy marvelous genius, perfect as the sun,
  Gave light and vigor to the Roman gloom;
  Europe to hold thy legions had not room;
Thy boundless mind craved worlds to overrun.

Thy will that shrank not at the Rubicon,
  Could in grave council virtues new assume,
  And while thy glory on the earth did bloom,
Proud nations hailed the grand deeds thou hadst done.

Thy clarion name will to all men recall
  The lofty soul, the valor undismayed!
We see thee battling 'mid the groves of Gaul,
  And when in robes Imperial arrayed,
Near Pompey's threatening marble thou didst fall,
  Supremely scorning thy assassins' blade!

LOUIS XII.

FRANCE.

Your joyous youth, when heedless of a crown,
　Passed amid laughing damoisels and flowers,
　Awed in grim Plessis, free in Touraine's bowers,
Loving to love, dreading a tyrant's frown!

Man of most nervous beauty and renown,
　You knew the torture of eventless hours,
　When from the gloom of Bourge's antique towers,
You desolate, gazed upon the dismal town.

But fate broke down your bars, and you were king
　Of that white, perfect pearl of nations, France,
　　Loved by its people, lord and liege thereof.
Ah why, when war by you had lost its sting,
　When your sweet life could crush its stern advance,
　　Why, lecherous graybeard, did you die,—of love?

CALIGULA.

ROME.

Imbecile brute, monster of blood and crime,
  A revel of slaughter, infamy and pain,
  Was't thy atrocious, grand and impious reign
That soiled the laurels of Cæsar in Rome's shrine.

Yet what a marvelous festal life sublime!
  Oceans of gore did the arenas stain;
  With what imperial pride thou didst disdain,
In rapine, incest, lust, the Fates and Time.

But history in its calm, impartial page,
  Has doomed thy deeds to an undying shame,
But I, a dreamer, doubt the impeccable sage,
  And openly avow I love thy name,
For in this vile and more degenerate age,
  I find no sinners worthy of thy fame.

RICHARD III.

ENGLAND.

Miraculous genius, grasping at the whole!
  Gossiping history calls you cruel, mad.
  Was not your hump enough to make you bad,
Politic despot ?   Aye, with bitter soul,

You played a grand and most stupendous rôle;
  Numbing your secret nature, good and glad,
  To juggle with crowns as does with stones a lad,
And wade through blood to a stupendous goal!

Brave, cunning, reckless, on broad Bosworth field,
  Where red swords gleamed, when Death claimed you his
      own,
You did not falter Richard, nor did yield,
  Or hear again the smothered prince's moan.
No victim-ghosts before your mind's eye reeled.
  What your grand soul regretted was a throne!

QUEEN ELIZABETH.

ENGLAND.

Poor foolish virgin that foreswore Love's creeds
  While a warm harlot heart throbbed strong with lust,
  Uncloyed, it soured thy bosom with mistrust,
Prompting thy mind to base and cruel deeds.

With limitless power, vast as thy jealous greeds,
  Thine iron hate no sympathy could rust,
  When thy hand, tremulous with rage unjust,
Doomed Mary's beauty in pale widow weeds.

Horrible proof of thy despotic power,
  I see the heated steel for suffering backs;
Whene'er I think of thee, the sullen Tower
  Looms up thro' winter fogs—I hear the racks
Creak for fresh victims at the fatal hour,
  And dream of Essex and a shining axe.

CHARLES VII.

FRANCE.

Improvident king that failed to make a mark,
   Poor moth that fluttered in the Saxon light,
   Heedless of armored foes that burn and smite,
To Honor's voice thy dull ear would not hark!

The valorous deeds of leal Joan of Arc,
   Rouse not thy dormant energy to the fight;
   The star of France swoons in the sullen night,
Chivalry sleeps, and the dire future's dark!

Thrice blesst be she within whose bosom burned,
   The sacred love of liberty, whose spell
Prompted thee on to laurels yet unearned!
   Who gave thee power, and her sweet love as well.
Hail to that woman, the world to praise has learned,
   Ravishing, white-browed, lofty-souled Sorel!

VISTAS AND LANDSCAPES.

ENGLAND.

A thousand thrifty towns on hill and plain,
   Dot with dark walls green leagues of meadows fair,
While blended seas majestic ever strain
   To guard their noble isle with deathless care.

Deep in the verdurous valley-lands of Kent,
   Fragrant with grain and odorous with flowers,
Blithe, buxom maidens when the day is spent,
   Dance on the velvet sward all gemmed with bowers

While herds of cattle browse in tangled woods,
   Which Ariel or Titania might have known,
And gypsies tread manorial solitudes,
   Where once shrill Saxon clarions were blown!

In castles old, that time and mold defy,
   The spirits of the Past with weird regrets,
May dream, as fire-fed engines rattle by,
   Of vanished Tudors and Plantagenets,

While where the slow Thames indolently flows,
   Lending to sooty piles its sluggish grace,
Lies mammoth London with its joys and woes,
   The panting heart of a colossal race!

On every side through all this busy land,
   In thymy glade, or in the city's moil,
Is ever heard exultingly the grand,
   Incessant harmony of incessant toil.

And from its wealthy, boisterous ports each day,
   With glorious pennants to the winds unfurled,
Gigantic ships sail haughtily away,
   Heralds of peace or war unto the world!

NORWAY.

High o'er the fjords and desolate pines the glow
  Of red auroras, like a golden fan,
Falls on the herbless wastes of Norway's snow,
  O'er lands that never knew the foot of man!

The maelstrom thunders on the craggy coasts,
  Blue icebergs wander in the solemn night;
While the grim glaciers, like gigantic ghosts,
  Loom with their white peaks in the spectral light.

Bleak moors spread out deserted, chill and lone;
  The wailing rooks whir cold wings on the shore;
While o'er the boundless wilds of fir and stone
  The frost-elves revel and the cataracts roar!

The land knows not the charm of birds that sing,
  No blossom of buds, no lithe and agile deer;
Unsought, uncared for, in mute suffering
  It bides its time, impassable and drear!

While the aurora, like a fiery flower,
  Blooms o'er the sterile leagues where none have trod,
And, in the awful silence of the hour,
  Dreams of its grandeur and communes with God!

ANDALUSIA.

The Alhambra, like a sculptured dream of stone,
   Lifts its pale marble to the drooping stars,
And near its august pillars overthrown,
   The wild gitanos thrum their soft guitars.

It seems the moon sheds milder, meeker rays
   Upon its maze of arabesques and signs,
In recollection of majestic days,
   When Moslem grandeur sanctified its shrines.

The very roses in the glamoured night
   Sigh for the Crescent and the conquered Moor;
To them the valiant Cid, in armored might,
   Freed not his beauteous Spain, but left it poor.

The pomp of Abderam, the caliph's courts,
   The glittering mosques, the festivals supreme,
The nights of song, the gladiatorial sports,
   All, all have vanished like a formless dream.

Cordova's gloom reveals the wondrous past,
   White Mihrabs tell of glorious epochs flown,
And Seville's Alcazars, superbly vast,
   Breathe of the mighty dead in every stone!

But sorrow has fallen on this sun-loved land;
  The hearts it cherished have been banished hence;
And now, bereft of Art's restoring hand,
  It slowly dies in its magnificence!

PALESTINE.

Where once two insolent cities Heaven defied,
  Hurling their woeful sins into its face,
There swooned a foully turgid, Lethean tide,
  While outraged Nature shuddered from the place.

But now, rich, fruitful orchards greet the eye;
  The sin of yore, purged by a sacred birth,
No longer stains the sapphire of the sky,
  Nor checks the roses smiling through the earth.

A lucent star shone in the expectant East,
  A God-loved land breathed with an unknown pride,
And from the manger of a humble beast,
  A holy name in Bethlehem was cried!
*   *   *   *   *   *   *
I roam amid this bounteous, beauteous land,
  Glittering in verdure, rare in oil and palm;
A blessing rests upon its cedars grand,
  A saintlike peace pervades its valleys' calm.

But in each lily, in each wavering stem,
  A loftier value my rapt fancies see;
Those wayside thorns were once a diadem,
  That blood-red rose dreams of Gethsemane!

Strangely oppressed, where'er I chance to fare,
   I see on olive branch and tufts of moss,
Haunting the ground, or in the weird, blue air,
   The awful, luminous shadow of a cross.

SWEDEN.

The trailing ivy blent with boreal flowers,
  Girdles with many a weird and leafy rune,
Thy sombre lakes, and the medieval towers
  Of Gripsholm, glittering in the icy moon.

The bleak, dull mountains yield their precious stores;
  Fertile and fair is Dalecarlian soil;
And calmly, on thy calm eves, by the shores
  Of Weners' sullen waves, thy peasants toil.

Upsal in granite grandeur sternly blooms,
  A flower of sculpture, where the rooks in throngs,
Haunt the gray niches and the gargoyle's glooms,
  Awed by the passing students' jocund songs.

Stockholm thy proud metropolis is gay
  With sounds of commerce and the rush of men,
And in thy groves where Bellman loved to stray,
  The Sagas of the past arise again.

I see thy puissant Charles with haughty glaive
  Haste to the Russ, and with his phantom hand
He seems to bid King Wasa, old and grave,
  Join his impetuous and victorious band!

Frithiof the Hero, Linnæus the most wise,
   Gigantic ghosts of everlasting fame
Pass rapidly before my marveling eyes,
   When memory, Sweden, calls thy honored name.

These will suffice thee as the days go by,
   This glorious pleiad that the world still stirs;
Now that thou dream'st below thine ashen sky,
   Wrapped in the dismal mantle of thy firs!

SCOTLAND.

The dull sun peers through foggy clouds, that flock
    Like sable phantoms, flecked by transient rays,
And colors with dun gold some tranquil loch,
    Whose blue heart blooms amid entangling braes.

Yonder the peak of Nevis towers in air,
    And glacially serene the sunlight spurns;
While at its base the blue-bells everywhere
    Are culled by kilted children singing Burns.

The sky is dappled now with amethyst,
    And from the mountain eeries you descry
Nebulous shapes and fancied forms of mist,
    The ghosts of Ossian's songs that seaward fly.

Below, within the thrifty dorp at work,
    The droning sound of bagpipes greets the ear;
While the grave bells in the old crumbling kirk
    Boom o'er the land their deep-lunged anthems clear.

No yearning, alas, is for the grand past felt,—
    The days of war and passion long have fled;
Men live indifferent as their fathers dwelt,
    Forgetting Scotia's great and noble dead!

And in the silent glens the giant oaks,
 Burdened with memories, wave no boughs in joy;
They who have felt great Bruce's claymore strokes,
 They who have heard the wild call of Rob Roy!

MEXICO.

Nature has lavished her most gorgeous dyes
    Upon the sunny beauty of thy groves;
Where many a bird, an airy opal, flies,
    And where the lithe and spotted puma roves.

Color, in pomp, reigns master of the land,
    Dazzling in rich supremacy of powers,
Dowering with deepest grace thy fertile strand,
    And reveling in the warm tint of thy flowers.

But over this magnificence, and all
    The life and radiance of thy forests vast,
There seems to hang, like some etherial pall,
    A shadow of the splendor of the past

When with a retinue of feathered Lords,
    Great Montezuma, stern and diamond-clad,
Rode to the Temples thro' the city's hordes,
    When Tenochtitlan by his sight was glad.

The free, glad time before the spoiler came,
    Cortez, irradiant in his burnished mail,
To doom great Guatamozin to the flame,
    And mar the town with storms of iron hail.

When Quetzacoatl's shrine was still adored,
  When Huitzilpotchli's glance was sought in dread,
And when each teocallis was begored
  By hosts of Aztec and Tlascalan dead!

Alas, these ferial days of loud display,
  These matchless epochs of imperial might
Have passed like thin and sun-pierced mist away,
  Leaving oblivion and thy starry night!

While Popocatapetl, grim and mute,
  With dull and sullen crater, mourns alone,
For that great Past sublime and absolute,
  Guarding the arcana of a race unknown!

GREECE.

A sun that seems to yearn for something dead
   Beams sullenly; the dull winds scarcely stir;
A marble column in a ravine's bed,
   Towers its decaying Doric chapiter.

A ruined temple, miracle of art,
   Where once assembled Dian's virgin bands,
Crumbles to dust, and in its haunted heart,
   Expectant crouch the swart, alert brigands.

There in the many-altared groves of old,
   The birds forget their Greek and dare not sing;
And 'mid the bowers where thoughtful Plato strolled,
   The slumberous flowers know no awakening.

The soul has fled of leaf, of bud and bird,
   There lurks no feeling in the giant trees
That shade the shattered statues, and have heard
   The rich, rare laugh of Aristophanes!

They dream in languorous ways, bereft, unsouled,
   Too proud to die, too haughty to complain,
And the sad sun, like a great tear of gold,
   Weeps for the Greece it ne'er shall light again!

INDIA.

Ganges swoons rippleless in the fierce mid-day,
   Drenched in the white-hot sun's acutest fires,
Winding in calm its turgid, indolent way,
   Around Benares and its thousand spires.

The monstrous crocodiles on either bank
   Loll in the sheen, and watch the ichneumons creep;
And 'mid the rushes, and the tall grass rank
   Of fecal pools, the huge flamingoes sleep.

No sound, no stir, no pleasant tip of oars,
   No sail to charm the scene, no cloud of white;
Naught but the silence of the scorching shores,
   Naught but the wilderness of burning light!

Master and slave have sought the shadeless' town,
   The iris fish hide in the alga dense,
With deadly heat the hell-sun poureth down,
   Blinding a continent in its insolence!

While o'er the slumbering waste of heat and sand,
   Where nothing human moves, o'r sways, or speaks,
Far in the fertile distance, mute and grand,
   Rise the great Himalayas' icy peaks!

ICELAND.

Like some calm, haughty man whose proud mien shows
　　An icy heart, concealing fierce desires,
So, in thy bosom of perpetual snows,
　　Oh mighty Hecla, dost thou hide thy fires!

The sibilant Geysers spout between the rocks
　　And mock thy silence through the sullen hours,
Thy languid spleen responds in feeble shocks,
　　But crushed and mute seem thy terrific powers.

About thy base, bare woodlands greet the eye,
　　Bouldered and firred, but desolately dead,
That once re-echoed with the Norsemen's cry,
　　And shook beneath the Vikings' iron tread!

But now the weird, sad Eddas of thy past
　　No more by Scalds are sung on moor and crick,
And all the memories of thy prowess vast
　　Fade in the smoky huts of Reijkiavik.

And crumbling walls upon thy ragged shores
　　Alone remind us of that troublous time
When Thangbrand's fleet urged by a thousand oars,
　　Brought to thy wolds Christ's messages sublime.

HOLLAND.

WINTER.

Amsterdam harbors full a thousand barks,
  Waifs from far southland, or pale Arctic sea,
And like some giant glow-worm's moving sparks,
  Their red lamps flicker on the Zuyder Zee.

The day is dull with rime and dense with snow;
  The busy burghers with a cleaving skate
Dart, like furred misty phantoms, to and fro
  O'er broad canals that crack beneath their weight.

Beyond, old wind-milled Zaandam, wrapped in gloom,
  Peers through the fog, and seems to guard the town,
But naught within the desolate gardens bloom,
  And on the icy meres no sun slants down.

Rigid and cold the huge metropolis stands,
  Stricken with sleet, yet longing for one bird
Of spring to bear it songs from fairer lands;
  But its sad, mute appeal is left unheard,

Save when some vessel, late from sun-loved isles,
  Keels its proud way up through the gulfs of ice,
To bathe grim Amsterdam in Orient smiles,
  And bring mock summer with a scent of spice.

PARIS.

Queen among cities, arrogantly fair,
  Brilliant with life thro' all thy broad expanse;
Thou art of beauty what men hold most rare—
  Oh, wonderful aorta of great France!

Art blooms in flower upon thy fecund breast;
  Thy warm, alluring voice greets one and all,
And in dark hours, when nations are oppressed,
  Or famine reigns, it is to thee they call.

Science and Song, Wit, Progress, Grace and Powers,
  Are thine and ever emanate from thee;
Thy streets are bathed in blood or decked with flowers—
  Thou makest slaves, thou grantest liberty.

Pleasure has made thee its enduring home;
  Alike thou art adored by boor and king;
And when upon thy humblest ways we roam
  Life seems more fair and Death doth lose its sting.

A Circe—strange and terrible—thou art!
  With charms as black as hell, as mad as mirth;
But even thy crimes seem sweet unto the heart—
  Thy smiles and sins alike delight the earth.

Thou art the perfect Eden of the eyes,
  The Paradise of senses and of moods;
Thou art the strange chameleon of surprise,
  With nameless noises and sad solitudes.

But sometimes, marvelous town, thou dost assume
  A wilder shape, and then the world, dismayed,
Sees, rising in the midnight's angry gloom
  The ominous shadow of the barricade.

EAST RUSSIA.

The domes of Nijni through the Volga's fog,
   Shoot toward the sun strange curvings Byzantine,
And like the giant shoulders of Magog,
   Uprear their massive bulk into its sheen.

Around the gates, tainting the early air,
   Roams with wild oaths a hideous moujik band,
Dragging their teas and cottons to the fair,
   To trade for costly silks of Samarcand.

Beyond spread out unfrozen steppes, still bare
   Though Spring has tipped with warmth the hueless grass,
Where Asian boors and Europe's ruffians share,
   In boisterous glee, some foaming bowl of qvass.

A sick and palsied sun illumes the scene;
   The river rumbles with its many ships;
Out from the town sway fields that scarce are green,
   Within, ring ballads from inebriate lips.

While on the desert wastes of gloom near by,
   No joyous home, no roadside flowers are found,
Naught but the uncertain sun, the sullen sky,
   And gaunt firs shivering on the barren ground.

While there, far in the distance, rude men goad
  A few pale Polish martyrs with hard blows,
And force their bleeding feet upon the road
  That leads to Death, or to Siberian snows.

CHINA.

Upon the rippleless Hoang-ho glides
  An uncouth junk with opium-eating crew.
Beyond, on distant dreamy river-sides,
  Slumber quaint cots and hamlets of bamboo.

Gaunt groups of Mongel soldiery, living bronze,
  Chant on the lower decks their guttural lays;
And through their midst some closely-shaven bonze
  Chews his betel and murmurs Buddha's praise.

Above, a haughty mandarin lolls and dreams
  Within the shade, while slaves wave colored plumes
To waft the cool air on his brow, that seems
  Furrowed and darkened by strong vinous fumes.

Near him, a maiden, almond-eyed and wee,
  Smiles at the river's azure vistas grand,
Daintily sipping aromatic tea,
  Her favorite parrot perched upon her hand.

The port is seen; like one diaphanous star,
  Kaifung, in all the argent of its kiosks,
Looms with its porcelain turrets from afar,
  'Mid huge pagodas and sweet-smelling bosks.

The gaudy sails vibrate, then fall and swoon,
   The ponderous anchor drops amid the stream,
And in the opal of the rising moon,
   I see great golden-dragoned banners gleam.

ARABIA.

Across red, sultry leagues of burning land,
  An arid terror and the dread of man,
Wearily crawls through seas of blistering sand,
  The straggling groups of a great caravan.

With dates and doura from the Yemen's shore,
  It braves the pitiless desert's fiercest heat;
The thirsty camels totter, faint and sore,
  The suffering Bedouins dream of cisterns sweet.

The road is long, and no refreshing palm
  Charms the infecund waste with verdant plumes;
The death-sun tortures them, the awful calm
  Angrily hints of imminent simooms.

Mecca, the wonder, with its bright, broad walls,
  Has been the goal that they will never reach,
And every hot and savage ray that falls,
  Is doomed their fated skeletons to bleach.

No more shall these poor wanderers behold
  The holy Caaba, and the sacred shrine,
Where, in a maze of marble and of gold,
  The Prophet slumbers in his rest divine.

Nor shall their balsams, myrrh and precious stones
   Be sold through Djedda's intricate bazaars.
And none will hear the muezzin when he drones
   The throng to Mosque below Medinian stars.

Shrieking to heedless Allah, sore afraid,
   By wafts of maddening, cruel heat o'erpowered,
In graves of shifting sand they will be laid,
   By ravenous swarms of locusts be devoured.

While o'er their scorched and withered bodies, strewn
   In disarray amid deserted tents,
The irreproachable and callous moon,
   Will rise in her serene magnificence.

PORTUGAL.

The warm and fecundating sunlight shines
   Down from the changeless azure of the sky,
On tangled leagues of olive groves and vines,
   Edens of verdure to the ravished eye.

Lisbon, all mantled in suave orange bloom,
   Smiles by the sea through calm and idle hours,
Oblivious to the days of woe and gloom,
   When earthquakes shattered Lusitanian towers.

While fair Oporto, girdled by great ships,
   Prepares its nectar for the expectant earth,
Delicious temptress of voluptuous lips,
   That mingles sorrow in the cup of mirth.

But ah, rare Portugal, the highly prized,
   Thou art no longer the chivalric land
That Camoens in his song immortalized,
   And which a Gama made sublimely grand.

Once peer of Spain, thy puissance now has fled;
   Wrested from thee is India proud and vast,
And all the tears thy glorious poets shed,
   Cannot revive the marvels of thy past.

And, as upon thy murmurous hills I dream,
 Each tree and flower in sorrow seems to yearn
For that illusive future day supreme
 When mighty Dom Sebastian will return.

EGYPT.

A sea of sand, dotted with date and palm,
   Rolls to the august Nile each scorching wave,
Where, in ineffable, eternal calm,
   Great pensive sphinxes crouch, sedate and grave.

Enormous crocodiles loll in the heat,
   Blue swallows nest in solemn Memnons' pschent,
And in a dreamy rest, serene and sweet,
   Tired camels browse before some Mameluke's tent.

Southward the skeleton of Memphis lies
   With granite vertebræ that dare the sun,
And through its mute and mighty remnant flies
   The famished jackal when the day is done.

Land of pyramidal pomp, of festal days,
   Of love, of lotus and divine carouse,
Dim centuries rob thy colcothar of praise,
   Now censers waft no myrrh upon thy brows.

No more from stately Thebes unto the seas,
   Are prayers for Anubis or to Isis said.
Proud land of kingly genealogies,
   And monstrous tombs, all song must call thee dead.

While in the noiseless night, with saddest ray,
   Thy melancholy moon, O Egypt, glows,
And over Karnac's arrogant decay,
   Dreams of the grandeur of dead Pharaohs.

IRELAND.

The gold, cloud-tossing sun with risen rays,
  Shakes from its face the morning's misty pall,
And gilds the gray, tempestuous sea, that plays
  Below the beetling cliffs of Donegal.

The mammoth causeway, weird with echoes dread,
  In basalt grandeur arrogantly looms,
Guarding the secrets of great races dead,
  Full of strange shadows and Titanic tombs.

Southward the sleepy Shannon idly flows,
  Where ruined towers and shattered hovels lie;
And in green vales enamored of the rose
  The sons of kings in squalor live and die!

Gone are the days when on thy mighty brow,
  O Ireland, shone the crown of powers sublime!
Deep in Killarney's liquid sapphire now
  Thy hopes and past have sunken for all time.

Yet thou art beautiful and noble still,
  Giving thy purest blood even in distress;
And of the lion England, by thy will,
  Thou hast become the bride and lioness.

But I who dream and dally in the past
  Love to revive again the time long fled,
When thy great chieftains through their forests vast
  The hardy Celtic legions foeward led.

And after, Erin, in my mind I see
  Doomed in a rain of lead and clash of blades,—
A valorous nation striving to be free,
  And redcoats lurking in the silent glades.

M

PERSIA.

A world of radiant roses, far and wide,
  Clasps in its red embiace fair Ispahan,
Which like a veiled and flower-wooed virgin bride,
  Blushes behind her santal-smelling fan.

Looped on the Zandrood's stream the city lies,
  A marvel of marble, whose white minarets,
One maze of arabesque, assault the skies,
  Until the admiring sun, reluctant, sets.

There, through yon open palace window, hear
  The satrap's favorites chatting with their birds;
Tuned to the low Kinoors, young voices clear,
  Warble sweet Saadi in soft Persian words.

One dainty houri tips each lash with khol,
  While eunuchs comb her tresses' liberal jet,
And with henné-stained fingers almées roll
  The fragrant, gold Latakieh cigarette.

Pale Schiraz buds adorn each silk divan,
  Odors of benzoin scent the morning air;
And tales from Hafiz or the Gulistan.
  Are softly syllabled by poets there.

And as I watch these fair Badouras play
   In drowsy grace, with amulets and curls,
I see in fancy, pass this sunny way,
   Some young Aladdin, scattering gold and pearls!

SUMATRA.

Land of warm dawns, and pestilential hours,
  Of lurid storms and tangled jungles dense;
A pomp of color stains thy mammoth flowers,
  Thy foliage gleams in gorgeous insolence.

Deep in the gloom of boas, thy upas white
  Spreads all its morbid branches to the sky,
While near thy weird rafflesias, in the night,
  The supple, monstrous tigers lurk and lie.

Gray mists malarial shelter from the sun
  Green Ophir's fruitful forests, where the red
And agile Kanchils timorously run
  Before the elephant's great thunderous tread.

Thy children, through the perilous glades and vast,
  Hunt the shy game and shun the cobra's fang;
Or, in long bark canoes they traverse fast,
  The blue and caiman-haunted Palembang.

Atrocious plague has found in thee a home,
  Unpitying as the reptiles in thy leaves;
Death lurks exultant in thy river's foam,
  Death flies on dark wings in thy sultry eves.

And Nature in some strange and savage mood,
 Implacably, I think, created thee,
To show to men, bewildered and subdued,
 How wonderful, and fearful she could be.

TURKEY.

The Bosphorus laves, in soft and sapphire calm,
    The cypressed shores, and courts the roses there,
With idle wave, craving a kiss of balm
    To waft in fragrance on the drowsy air.

Frail, on the blue tides speed the gaudy caïques,
    Swift as the gulls that hasten through the night,
Striving to reach, before the Muezzin strikes,
    Stamboul, in all its glory and its light.

Beyond, arise the argent and the gold
    Of myriad minarets, shimmering in the glow
Of the great couchant sun, in purple rolled,
    That lingers o'er them and seems loath to go.

Below, the city awaits the coming stars.
    The lamps are trimmed amid the radiant Kiosks;
Vast, turbaned throngs swarm thro' the loud bazaars,
    And Imans chant within the domèd mosques.

While in yon marble palace, rising grand
    Above the fig and orange of its grove,
A young slave dreams of her Circassian land,
    And sighs in vain for liberty and love.

SWITZERLAND.

Down from thine icy mountains' towering heights,
   White shrines of God, where man would fain adore
Forever in the star-encumbered nights,
   The thunderous avalanches whirl and roar.

Deep in thy valleys by wild winters tried,
   Scions of men who warred at Morat dwell;
Men in whose simple, noble hearts abide
   The sacred names of Sempach and of Tell.

Near tranquil Zurich's sapphire lake, where once
   Lacustrian races lived and loved and fought,
The hardy peasant the lithe chamois hunts,
   Or tracks the mighty bears to lairs unsought.

The agile ibex darts about thy rocks
   Where fearless eagles scream and sunward fly,
Scorning the glittering glacier's angry shocks,
   Far over beetling peaks that time defy.

Here, mantled everywhere by dismal firs,
   I see grim chasms and precipices vast,
Haunted by weird and ghostly worshipers;
   Where Manfred raved, and where Napoleon passed.

And thy green vales where battles have been born,
　Mute witnesses of many a glorious deed,
Can yet remember Gessler's haughty scorn,
　And echo still the cry of Winkelried.

While over all, bewildering and grand,
　Serene in lurid lights and awful glooms,
Chaste guardian of this pure, heroic land,
　In flawless majesty the Jungfrau looms.

ITALY.

A queen of nations, in serenest pride,
   Unique, invincible, thou risest now;
The unsheathed sword of freedom by thy side,
   A crown resplendent on thy affluent brow!

Rarer with brilliants circled in its gold,
   Brighter by far than elder diadems,
Glitter and flash before the world grown old,
   The splendors of these congregated gems.

Venice! wave-loved and haunted by the stars,
   Somberly dreams its life and love away,
Wrapped in a lethargy that nothing mars,
   Haughty and sad in its superb decay.

Naples! a sunny maiden, warm with wine,
   Smiles amid vine-wreathed bowers and luscious fruit,
While like some treacherous Satan saturnine,
   Fretful Vesuvius guards her, grimly mute.

Genoa! a maze of marble and of mould,
   Swoons in the clutches of the avid priest,
Forgetful of the prowesses of old.
   When DORIA'S galleys terrorized the East.

Verona! labyrinth of tortuous lanes,
    That shield the virginal snow of many doves;
Proud in the fragrance of its pregnant plains,
    Guarding immortal tombs, immortal loves.

Florence! coquettish in its robe of vines,
    Jests like a page enamored of itself,
And with excess of melodies and wines,
    Drowns the black past of Ghibelline and Guelf.

Pisa! in priestly garb, with sullen streets,
    The sad *far niente* of mediæval stone;
Stern in its dim, monastical retreats,
    With marvel-seeds upon its piazze sown.

Milan! the beautiful, that laughs at care,
    In all the rapture of her birdful Mays;
A modern siren, blithe and debonair,
    Charming the world with light Bellinian lays.

While *Rome*, majestic, solemnly fulfills
    Its sacerdotal sovereignty immense;
Displaying from the green, historic hills,
    Its indestructible magnificence.

These are thy gems, oh *Italy*, and fast
    Before my mind thy dazzling annals show
The consecrated giants of the past,
    BOCCACCIO, DANTE, PETRARCH, ANGELO!

And with prophetic gaze, all eyes can see
   Thy peerless future dawning, proud and grand,
When great and indefectible, and free,
   Supreme among the nations thou wilt stand.

BURGUNDY.

Delicious land whose fields are fair with trees,
   Whose liberal rivers lave a lavish soil,
Bloom on amid thy flowerful mysteries,
   Where Nature labors without pain or toil.

The sun has blessed thee and his beams escape
   In fecund ways, effulgent and benign,
To kiss with color thy rich, juicy grape,
   And tinge with gold the glory of thy vine.

Silenus hides him in thy maze of leaves,
   Prompting thy tendrils to be lithe and sweet;
Soft, in the silence of red Autumn eves,
   I hear the drowsy shuffle of his feet.

While dews invisible descend through night,
   To cool thy vineyards from the enamored sun,
Great domes of stars that burn with gorgeous light,
   Complete the beauty that they shine upon.

LAPLAND.

From northern fjords, a souvenir of snow,
    Long, frigid nights and dismal landscapes grim,
When I in Lapland dwelt long years ago,
    Haunt my sad mind with pain no time can dim.

I never can forget the frozen moors,
    The drear, white, pine-lined steppes of glistening rime,
The damp, dull skies whose darkness still allures
    My fluctuant memory to that vanished time.

I see the houses hewn of icen blocks,
    Caressed by raging storms of wind and sleet;
I hear the White Sea murmur on the rocks,
    Sad, Boreal songs, melodiously sweet.

Out on the wastes, environed by the snow,
    My nomad Lapland friends find rest and homes,
While, far thro' night, I see the distant glow
    Of white Finn cities and their silver domes.

A wondrous tongue mellifluous I hear,
    A language surely I once spake before,
And lo! I see the slim and sturdy deer
    Drag a Kabitka o'er a barren shore.

And ah! can I forget my Finnish maid,
    That polar pearl, delicious and divine,
Who looked so glacial in her furs arrayed;
    Who was so loving with her lips to mine.

Ah no, the touch of her dead kisses, lost,
    Was sweeter than all kisses given to me;
Her heart's love budding in that land of frost,
    Was warmer than all tropic love could be.

And yet I left her to chagrins and woes,
    That solemn night when four great reindeer drew
My quivering sledge o'er leagues of hueless snows,
    Down the vague distances of freezing blue. . .

I left her on that silent midnight cold,
    To mourn for me, to weep for me, alone,
While over Lapland, like a fan of gold
    The red Aurora Borealis shone!

BRAZIL.

Broad, boundless forests, pure of human tread,
  Uprear luxuriant foliage to the sun,
And like a great, imperial mantle, spread
  Their green magnificence round the Amazon.

Here, like some giantess' bracelets, coiled
  Around huge trunks gorged anacondas sleep,
While through the stagnant pools, by rank weeds soiled.
  Grim, mottled saurians indolently creep.

Shunning no huntsman, the lithe pumas play,
  The chattering lories sparkle on the trees,
Sleek tapirs through the ferny quagmires stray,
  The pied sloths find uninterrupted ease.

All feel secure, no hurtling arrows speed
  To whirr destruction through the wondrous place,
And from majestic branch to humble weed
  All blooms untrammeled in primeval grace.

OTAHEITE.

Circled by coral, blessed with endless May,
  Beloved of birds, and fair with bud and palm,
O happy isle, thou liest far away,
  Like some sweet mirage of delicious calm.

With spice and yams thy plenteous valleys teem,
  Softly thy rippling rivers seaward wind,
And in thy tropic radiance thou dost seem
  A gem in the Pacific's heart enshrined.

Bold mountains rise exultant from thy breast,
  Cool cataracts from thy flowery ledges bound,
And all the blue intense of Heaven has blessed
  Thy green perfection by the sunlight crowned.

Within thy redolent glades alive with birds,
  A world of gorgeous leafage warmly blooms,
And in thy groves, with soft Malayan words,
  Dusk lovers chant their murmurous pantoums.

Oro, thy god of war, and Hiro stern,
  No more find worship on thy gory shrines;
No more will lamentable rites return
  To soil with blood thy sward of trailing vines.

Plenty and peace are thy reward to-day;
   Gone are the barbed spears, the pagan drum;
In fragrant pasture-lands meek cattle stray,
   On ruined temples the great wild bees hum.

Mute are the hideous idols thou didst praise,
   Adored, ere brave men compassing the earth
First found thee in the dead adventurous days,
   And to the attentive world proclaimed thy worth.

And now, transcendent with thy stormless skies,
   Dreamily fair, an Eden of the sea,
Thy beauty blooms before our ravished eyes,
   An image of what Paradise will be.

N